Tex the Explorer

Journey Around the Earth

For Lilah
Love Ellie

Written by Ellie Smith
Illustrated by Eyen Johnson

ISBN: 1723034142

ISBN13: 978-1723034145

This book is dedicated to our families.

Tex's family encourages and supports him.
Our families encourage and support us!

Happy Birthday Tex!

Tex loves to explore. For his birthday his parents gave him a new airplane.

Happy Birthday Tex!

Tex was on his way!

Tex decided to visit the seven continents of Earth.

Tex was on his way!

North America

Tex flew over Niagara Falls.

North America

Tex landed near the
Golden Gate Bridge.

South America

Tex flew over the Amazon River.

South America

Tex landed near Machu Pichu.

Europe

Tex flew over the Alps.

Europe

Tex landed near Big Ben.

Asia

Tex flew over Mount Fuji.

Asia

Tex landed near the
Great Wall of China.

Africa

Tex flew over the Serengeti
National Park.

Africa

Tex landed near the
Pyramids of Giza.

Australia

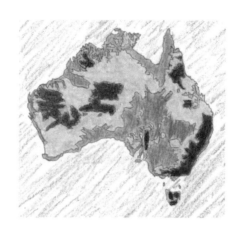

Tex flew over the Great Barrier Reef.

Australia

Tex landed near the
Sydney Opera House.

Antarctica

Tex flew over the ice.

Antarctica

Tex landed near a research station.

Tex decided it was time to fly home.

He had visited all seven continents.

Tex decided it was time to fly home.

Some Facts About the Earth

The Earth is the third planet from our sun.

The Earth is our home.

The Earth has seven continents: North America
South America
Europe
Asia
Africa
Australia
Antarctica

A continent is a huge area of land.

There are many countries on each continent.

Reading a Map

The different colors on the maps in this book tell you the about the land on each continent.

Map Key

Blue - Ice
Green - Lowlands
Yellow - Hills and Plains
Brown - Mountains

Ellie Smith is a retired special education teacher from Maryland, now living in Central Pennsylvania. She met Eyen Johnson when he was in kindergarten, and they first discussed creating a book together when he was in fifth grade. They published their first book together after Eyen graduated from high school.

This is the second book in their "Tex the Explorer" Series.

Tex the Explorer: Journey to Mars

Tex the Explorer: Journey Around the Earth

Awards Won by Tex
(With a Little Help from Ellie and Eyen)

Chanticleer International Book Awards Shortlist
Independent Press Award® Distinguished Favorite
indieBRAG® Medallion Honoree
Mom's Choice Awards® Silver Recipient
Purple Dragonfly Book Awards Winner
Royal Dragonfly Book Awards Winner
Story Monsters Approved®

Made in the USA
Middletown, DE
03 August 2021

45124324R00027